THE FIRE ENGINE BOOK

Pictures by
Tibor Gergely

A GOLDEN BOOK • NEW YORK

Copyright © 1950, 1959, renewed 1987 by Random House, Inc. All rights reserved.
Published in the United States by Golden Books, an imprint of Random House Children's
Books, a division of Random House, Inc., New York. GOLDEN BOOKS, A GOLDEN BOOK,
A LITTLE GOLDEN BOOK, the G colophon, and the distinctive gold spine are
registered trademarks of Random House, Inc.
ISBN: 978-0-375-84010-4
www.goldenbooks.com   www.randomhouse.com/kids
Educators and librarians, for a variety of teaching tools,
visit us at www.randomhouse.com/teachers
Library of Congress Control Number: 00109707

PRINTED IN CHINA

Ding, ding, ding! goes the alarm.

The firemen slide down the pole.

Clang, clang, clang! goes the fire engine bell.

The chief is on his way.

Here they come!

Watch out! Make way for the hose car.

Hurry, hurry! Jump on the hook-and-ladder truck!

The people come running out to see

the great big hook-and-ladder truck.

Here they are at the fire.

The chief tells his men what to do.

Quick! Connect the hoses!

S-s-s-s! goes the water.

Crank, crank. Up go the ladders.

Up go the firemen with their hoses.

Chop, chop, chop! go the axes.

Crash! go the windows.

Down the ladders come the firemen.

They jump into the net to save things from the fire!

Sput, sput, sput! Out goes the fire.

Tired firemen and people go home.

Hurray for the brave firemen!